WANTED:
Electron.

CRIMES:
Kidnapping.
Tyranny.
Dictatorship.

WHEREABOUTS:
Microworld.

YOUR MISSION:
Capture Electron and
rescue the planet!

Bantam Books in the
Be An Interplanetary Spy Series

BE AN INTERPLANETARY SPY™ 8

MISSION TO MICROWORLD

by Seth McEvoy
illustrated by Alex Nino
and Steve Fastner

A Byron Preiss Book

BANTAM BOOKS
TORONTO • NEW YORK • LONDON • SYDNEY • AUCKLAND

To Bebe Reitmeyer, my sister

Seth McEvoy, author, is an active member of the Science Fiction Writers of America; is a video game designer and programmer; has written a biocritical study of science fiction author Samuel R. Delany for Frederick Ungar, Publishers; has also written *How to Program Arcade Games on the Timex 1500 Computer* and *How to Program Arcade Games on the T199/4a Computer* for Compute! Books, and *Create-4-Game on the VIC-20* for Dell Books.

Steve Fastner and *Alex Nino* are fantasy artists whose work have appeared in other volumes of *Be An Interplanetary Spy.* They have also done illustrations for publishers such as Heavy Metal, Sal Q., Starlog and Marvel.

RL4, IL age 9 and up

MISSION TO MICROWORLD
A Bantam Book / November 1984

Special thanks to Ann Weil, Susan Hui Leung, Ron Buehl and Lisa Novak.

Cover art by Steve Fastner

Additional design and production by Susan Hui Leung

Cover design by Alex Jay
Series graphic design by Marc Hempel
"BE AN INTERPLANETARY SPY" is a trademark of Byron Preiss Visual Publications, Inc.

Typesetting by David E. Seham Association, Inc.

ISBN 0-553-24521-X

Published simultaneously in the United States and Canada

Bantam Books are published by Bantam Books, Inc. Its trademark, consisting of the words "Bantam Books" and the portrayal of a rooster, is Registered in U.S. Patent and Trademark Office and in other countries. Marca Registrada. Bantam Books, Inc., 666 Fifth Avenue, New York, New York 10103.

Printed and bound in Great Britain by Hunt Barnard Printing Ltd.

O   0 9 8 7 6 5 4 3 2 1

Introduction

You are an Interplanetary Spy. You are about to embark on a dangerous mission. On your mission you will face challenges that may result in your death.

You work for the Interplanetary Spy Center, a far-reaching organization devoted to stopping crime and terrorism in the galaxy. While you are on your mission, you will take your orders from the Interplanetary Spy Center. Follow your instructions carefully.

You will be traveling alone on your mission. If you are captured, the Interplanetary Spy Center will not be able to help you. Only your wits and your sharp Spy skills will help you reach your goal. Be careful. Keep your eyes open at all times.

If you are ready to meet the challenge of being an Interplanetary Spy, **turn to page 1.**

TOP SECRET

You are an Interplanetary Spy.
After capturing the rebel Spy Valeeta
on the planet Delbor and saying
goodbye to Callisto, you are cruising
through Sector 22 when your sub-
space radio picks up a galactic alert.
Write in your Interplanetary Spy ISBN
number below, to unscramble the
coded radio message:

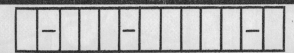

If you are not sure, check the back cover of this book.

Turn to page 2.

2 You unscramble the radio message. It is from another Interplanetary Spy!

The face on the screen is familiar, but there is a lot of static in the picture. You hear only a few words: "Danger . . . Spy Base . . . Parno . . . Send help . . . Electron. . . ."

It is the biodroid! You worked with him when you fought Marko Khen, the Galactic Pirate.

Go on to the next page.

The transmission stops.

Your friend the biodroid is in trouble. You must go to him. You quickly set your ship's navigation computer for the planet Parno.

Instantly your ship blasts into hyperdrive!

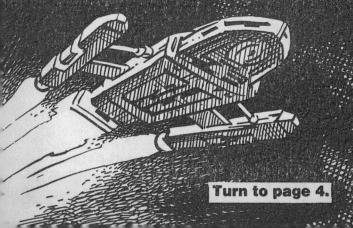

Turn to page 4.

You enter Sector 63 from hyperspace. Your navigation computer tells you that Parno should be in front of you.

But you see nothing on any of your screens!

Go on to the next page.

While your navigation computer rechecks the star positions to make sure there was no mistake, you read the data file on Parno.

**Data file 4-7-54
PARNO**

The planet Parno, orbiting the sun Vazil, in Sector 63, is a remote Interplanetary Spy training base. At present all Spy recruits assigned to Parno are on a secret training mission. The base is guarded by a single class 47-P biodroid.

Your navigation computer gives a report. Parno *should* be directly in front of you, but all you see is empty space.

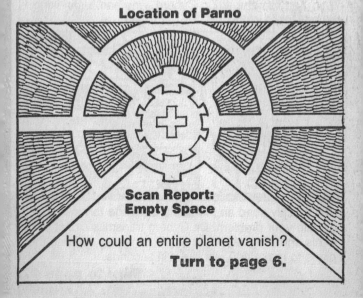

Location of Parno

**Scan Report:
Empty Space**

How could an entire planet vanish?

Turn to page 6.

This must be the tiny humanoids' world. The deadly energy beam came from here, so Electron must be here too. Could such a tiny planet contain any clue about the missing biodroid and the disappearance of the planet Parno? The only way to investigate is to make yourself smaller, but how?

Wait! You remember Dr. Cyberg, who had a shrinking ray on Robot World.

You quickly send an infraradio message to him. You explain your problem. Dr. Cyberg transmits circuit plans of his shrinking ray. Your ship's computer can use the plans to make one just like it in seconds.

Turn to page 17.

You move toward the left. As you get closer, the ship's scanners tell you that you are approaching an ion field.

ION FIELD OF PLANET PARNO

The fact that you are picking up an ion field tells you that the planet Parno *was* here, less than six hours ago, but it is gone now. What happened to Parno?

SEND HELP
ELECTRON
DANGER
GALAXY

You see something odd on your front viewscreen. It looks as if a message is forming. If so, the message is floating a few inches away from your ship! It's in a language you've never seen before.

Turn to page 12.

You decide to look for an ion ghost image, which may give you a clue about Parno's disappearance. All planets have an ion ghost image, even planets you can't see. You examine every screen.

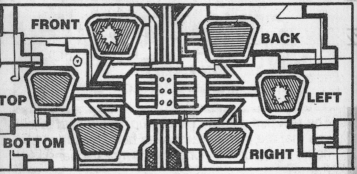

Two of the screens seem to have a faint image on them. You focus in more tightly.

LEFT VIEW

FRONT VIEW

Watch out! Black holes also look like ion ghost images. Ion ghost images have an *even* number of points and black holes have an *odd* number of points.

Move toward the left? Turn to page 7.

Move toward the front? Turn to page 10.

The computer translates the message by using the alphabet you picked.

Flonari Language:

BLAST PLANET NOW ELECTRON DANGER

The tiny humanoids seem to be asking you to blast a planet. Even if you can't see it, you can still blast whatever is in front of you. You fire.

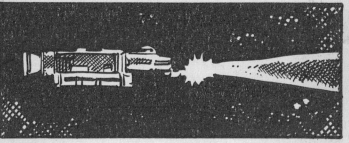

The energy blast bounces back! Your ship is torn apart by the force of the blast. You should have studied ancient languages more carefully, Spy!

The End

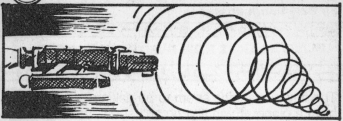

Something is wrong. Alarm bells ring as your hand reaches for the reverse thruster control. But you are too late! Your ship is being sucked into a black hole.

The ship moves through the black hole into ultra-space.

Suddenly your ship returns to normal space. Something has happened to your mind. *You don't remember a thing.* All you know is that you must . . .

Turn to page 1.

Before you can spell out a message to the tiny humanoids, an energy ray comes out of nowhere and blasts them!

Who would do such a thing? Since the humanoids were trying to warn you against Electron, Electron might have destroyed them.

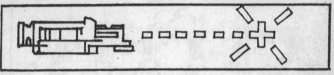

You get an idea. Since the humanoids were so tiny, maybe you can find out more if you scan space with your microscopic scanner. You can also use your computer to see where the deadly energy beam came from.

You see a tiny world!

Turn to page 8.

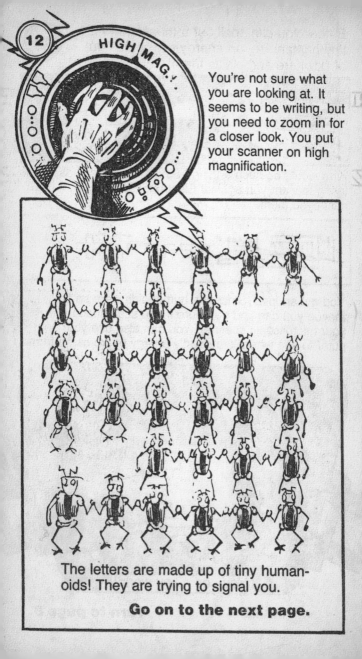

You use your computer language translator to see if you can find an alphabet that matches. If you can read the message, you may be able to find out more about the biodroid's danger.

The computer finds letters from two ancient alphabets that may match the message on the screen. Which letter matches the pattern that the tiny humanoids are making on the opposite page?

Flonari: B

Ackaroo: S

This one?
Turn to page 9.

This one?
Turn to page 16.

Tell the computer which alphabet you think the message is in.

You plug the boards together correctly. You are now ready to shrink yourself and your ship to the correct size.

How small should you shrink? You use a special microscanner, which is linked to the circuit boards. You scan the microworld at different magnifications. The scanner picks up two different planets in the same place! One is a lot bigger than the other.

This is the planet you see at a magnification of one million times.

This is the planet you see at a magnification of one billion times.

Which is the real microworld? You must pick one and set the controls to shrink yourself to that size.

Million times smaller?
Turn to page 18.

Billion times smaller?
Turn to page 22.

Hint: Which planet looks inhabited?

You fly in close and see that even if this world is microscopic, it has towns, mountains, rivers, and valleys.

You see a large, magnificent city. You decide to land here to begin your search for clues to the disappearance of the planet Parno and your friend the biodroid.

Turn to page 24.

The computer translates the message by using the alphabet you picked.

Ackaroo Language:

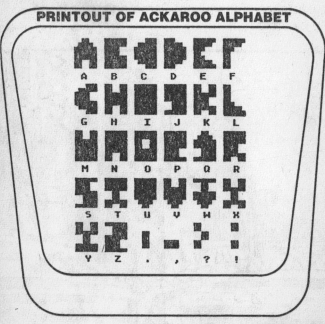

SEND HELP ELECTRON DANGER GALAXY

Electron? The only mention of the name Electron in your ship's data banks is the emergency message from the biodroid. Since the tiny humanoids mention Electron too, this may be a clue to the biodroid's disappearance.

Your ship's language computer prints out the rest of the Ackaroo alphabet so you can communicate with the tiny humanoids.

PRINTOUT OF ACKAROO ALPHABET

A B C D E F
G H I J K L
M N O P Q R
S T U V W X
Y Z . , ? !

Turn to page 11.

The ship's computer makes three circuit boards, which can shrink you and your ship to any size.

You must plug the boards into each other in the proper order to activate the shrinking ray. Hurry, before Electron blasts you the same way the tiny humanoids were blasted!

You look at the circuit boards:

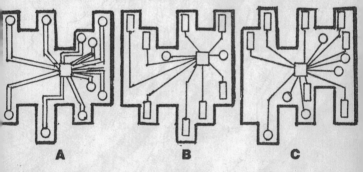

There is only one way for the uneven edges of the tops and bottoms of the boards to fit together perfectly. Do not turn the boards upside down.

B-A-C?
Turn to page 14.

C-B-A?
Turn to page 21.

18 You are now ready to investigate the microworld you have discovered. You activate the shrinking ray.

You and your ship get smaller and smaller. Dr. Cyberg explained that as your body shrinks, you will move faster. This will allow your body's energy to match its smaller size.

You see the microworld in your view-screen!

19

Turn to page 15.

You flew up when you should have flown down. One of the automatic tracking lasers gets you in its sights!

You try to dodge the laser beam.

But it is faster than you are!

The End

You plug the circuit boards together. The edges don't quite match, but you might as well give it a try.

You activate the power. Something is wrong! The ship is getting smaller, but you're not shrinking at all.

The circuit to shrink your body isn't working. Your ship is now too small to hold you. You burst out into space. Your suit protects you, but you have no way to get home. It's a long walk, Interplanetary Spy!

The End

You are now ready to investigate the microworld you have seen. You shrink a billion times!

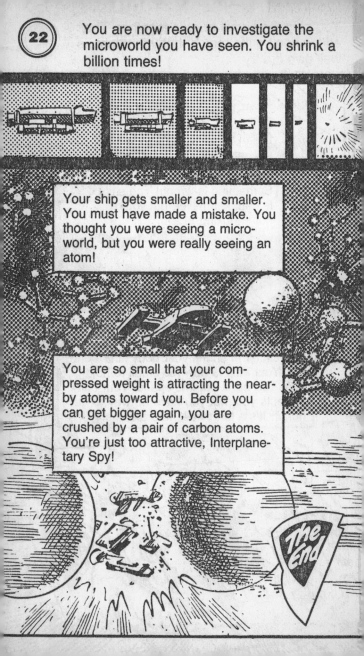

Your ship gets smaller and smaller. You must have made a mistake. You thought you were seeing a micro-world, but you were really seeing an atom!

You are so small that your compressed weight is attracting the near-by atoms toward you. Before you can get bigger again, you are crushed by a pair of carbon atoms. You're just too attractive, Interplanetary Spy!

The End

You begin to explore the city, but you notice something strange!

Everyone is moving at ultraspeed! Bodies look stretched out because they are moving faster than your eyes can see. Voices sound like chirping birds. Be careful!

Turn to page 26.

DANGER! ALERT!

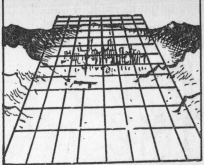

Your ship's scanner tells you that there is an invisible grid of death ray beams protecting the city. You can fly *over* the dark beams and *under* the light beams.

Also, automatic tracking laser cannons will blast you if you fly over two beams in a row, or under two beams in a row.

You can fly under these beams: ≡≡≡

You can fly over these beams: ▬▬▬

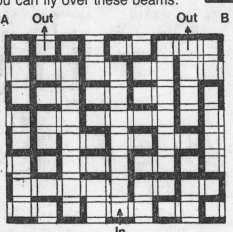

If you enter at the bottom, where will you come out? You can't go back once you start.

Position A? Turn to page 27.
Position B? Turn to page 20.

Remember: you can't go *over* or *under* two in a row.

You made a mistake! The figure you approached was a warrior, moving at superspeed. But he thinks you are a statue because it seems as if you aren't moving.

The warrior takes you to a park. Other warriors bring cement and pour it around your feet. You can't move fast enough to escape. You will remain here forever!

The End

There are two kinds of microworlders buzzing around you—warriors and citizens. The warriors carry spears and wear helmets. You hide before they run you down.

Look out! Two microworlders are moving near your hiding place, and they will see you. Which one should you trust?

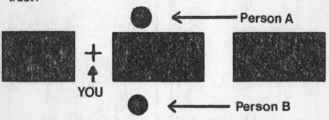

Here is what they look like. Which is *not* the warrior?

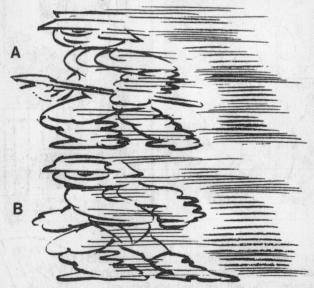

Person A? Turn to page 25.

Person B? Turn to page 30.

You dart over and under the invisible beams without being hit by the laser cannon. You are able to approach the city unseen.

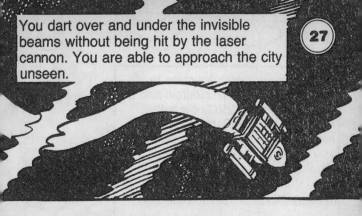

You land your ship in a park and get out.

Turn to page 23.

You can now search for clues to the disappearance of the biodroid and the planet Parno. All you know is that someone named Electron may be responsible. Before you go very far, you see a gigantic floating ship coming toward you!

It seems to be a castle in the sky!

Hiding behind a rock, you watch the floating castle come closer.

It is coming right toward you! How can the pilot know you are here?

Turn to page 37.

You made a wise choice, Spy! The citizen passes you without calling any warriors. You must speed yourself up. Since Dr. Cyberg's ray speeds up a person as it makes him smaller, you can adjust it so that it will make you go a little bit faster.

But how much faster should you go? Using your scanner, you are able to see how a microworlder would look if he were moving as slowly as you are now. How much wider is the top picture than the bottom?

8 times wider? Turn to page 33.
10 times wider? Turn to page 42.

Speed yourself up so that you can continue to search for clues!

You come to another part of the city and jump off the moving sidewalk.

You search the streets of the city. You must find someone you can trust, so that you can learn what Electron did to the biodroid and Parno.

You come to an alley. In it you find a microworlder who is injured. If you help him, he might tell you what you need to know.

Turn to page 32.

You examine the injured microworlder's head with your scanner.

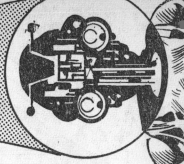

This body is more like a computer than a human! Instead of a brain it has a main central processor. Instead of lungs it has memory banks, and instead of a heart it has a power supply.

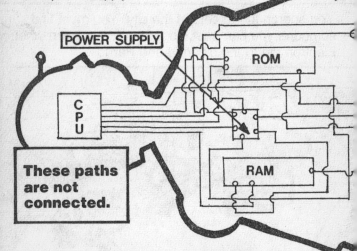

POWER SUPPLY

ROM

C
P
U

These paths are not connected.

RAM

To make it well again, you must analyze the body's circuits. How many electrical paths are there between the central processor and the power supply?

Two electrical paths? Turn to page 35.
Three electrical paths? Turn to page 38.

You activate Dr. Cyberg's ray and speed
yourself up eight times.

A

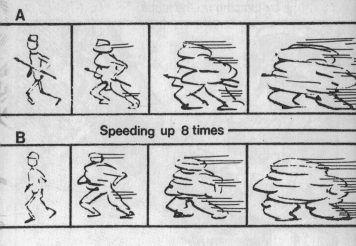

Speeding up 8 times

B

Warrior

Citizen

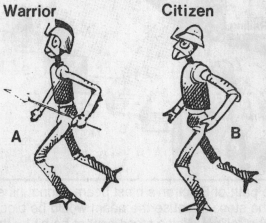

A

B

Now the microworlders look normal!

Turn to page 28.

One blast from Electron's trident would be fatal! You've got to get out of here. You see a moving sidewalk to the right. Maybe you can reach it by jumping up the steps.

The path of Electron's blast beam cannot hit some of the steps because the beam would be blocked by the railing. Which steps cannot be hit by the beam?

Steps A-D-F? Turn to page 41.

Steps A-C-E? Turn to page 36.

Hurry! Electron will fire any second!

You find only two paths between the central processor and the power supply. You pull out one of the wires to see if it is broken.

The wire is OK. But when you put it back, you cause a major short circuit! A million volts zap you. Maybe you should have studied more about computers when you had the chance!

The End

You escape Electron's energy blast! You leap onto the moving sidewalk and are quickly carried away.

Electron's floating castle moves too slowly to keep up with you. You have managed to outwit Electron temporarily, and you are even more sure that he is responsible for the disappearance of the planet Parno and your friend the biodroid.

Turn to page 31.

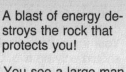

A blast of energy destroys the rock that protects you!

You see a large man with a trident and a helmet, sitting on a throne in the front of the castle. He speaks: "I am Electron. Who dares to enter my microworld?"

You do not answer fast enough. Electron laughs and says: "I found you by tracing your energy. Now I shall drain that energy from your bones, foolish intruder!" He raises his trident.

Turn to page 34.

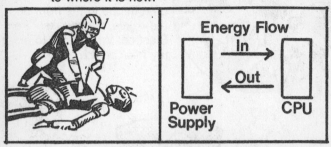

38 You see that there are three paths from the central processing unit to the power supply. Your knowledge of electricity tells you that there should only be two. One of the three doesn't belong there and must have accidentally shifted to where it is now.

Energy Flow

In →

← Out

Power Supply

CPU

You remove one of the wires and put it back where it belongs. The operation is a success! The microworlder sits up. He thanks you for saving his life.

Go on to the next page.

The microworlder tells you that his name is CEM-450. You ask him to tell you about Electron.

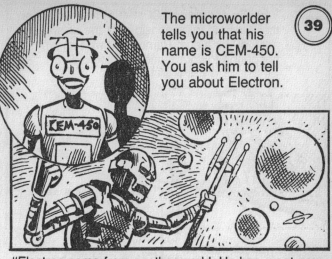

"Electron came from another world. He has great powers and was able to capture all our atomic energy reactors. But he needs so much energy that even our world cannot satisfy him.

"When we found out that he had captured a nearby giant world to feed on its energy, we sent for help. I am one of the leaders of the rebel forces against Electron."

You tell him that you are an Interplanetary Spy, and you promise to help him defeat Electron. CEM-450 tells you that he must rest now but you should meet him at the Interface Tavern on Romram Street in eight hours.

Turn to page 40.

You say goodbye to CEM-450. Now you know that Electron is responsible for the disappearance of the planet Parno. You wonder what happened to your friend the biodroid.

As you wander through the city, you notice a poster on a wall. The face on it has been partly burned away by chemicals.

The face reminds you of the biodroid, who has part of his head missing. Could the biodroid still be alive . . . and on this tiny planet?

Biodroid

Your scanner tells you that the burns on the poster were made by a chemical, which is *only* found in the body of the biodroid. He could have burned the poster to tell you that he is here.

Turn to page 44.

42 You activate Dr. Cyberg's ray and speed yourself up ten times.

Something is wrong! As you begin to move forward, you smell something burning. It is . . . you! You're moving so fast that you burst into flames. This isn't what you had in mind when you told people you were going to set the world on fire!

The End

You follow the trail of the posters. They lead to a sports arena.

Is the biodroid inside? You go through a doorway. Suddenly a grating drops behind you. You can't go back!

You go forward into the arena and see four fierce monsters inside. It's a trap!

You might be able to fight one or two monsters, but four? You are doomed!

The End

The biodroid may have left clues on other posters. You begin searching through the city, looking at each poster carefully. You are sure that the biodroid has been here, but you must be careful. It could be a trap.

Keep looking on the next page!

Which of the posters have been changed by the biodroid to give you clues?

Posters B-D-F? Turn to page 50.

Posters A-C-E? Turn to page 43.

Turn to page 40 to see a picture of the biodroid.

You go through the maze of tunnels and find the biodroid's cell. You hear music. The cell door opens and you walk inside.

The biodroid greets you warmly. "I knew you would come," he says. "We must stop Electron before he captures more planets."

Turn to page 52.

Just as you and the biodroid are about to leave, the doorway fills with warriors!

The cell door slams shut. You see a video screen on the wall. On it is the face of Electron.

Electron speaks: "Fool! You walked right into my trap. You'll rot in my prison until I'm ready to take your energy."

Turn to page 48.

You and the biodroid wait in the cell for a long time. There must be a way out. A warrior comes with the evening meal. But there are too many warriors with him for you to risk an attack.

If only you could grab the keys. . . . Wait! The warrior didn't *have* a key. He whistled a tune. Maybe you can unlock the door by whistling the same tune.

You whistle the same tune, but nothing happens.

Go on to the next page.

The biodroid speaks: "It's no use. He whistles a different tune each time." You think for a moment. Then you ask the biodroid if he remembers the last few tunes that the warrior whistled.

"These are the tunes," says the biodroid.

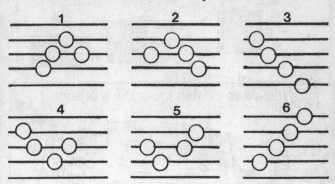

It might be a repeating pattern! You analyze it with your scanner. You get two tunes that may open the door. Which one would follow the last tune, if they are repeating?

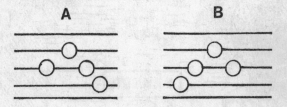

Tune A? Turn to page 56.

Tune B? Turn to page 53.

You follow the trail of the posters.

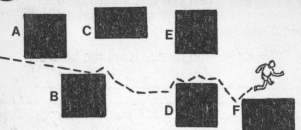

You come to what looks like a prison.

PRISON

The biodroid could be inside!

Go on to the next page.

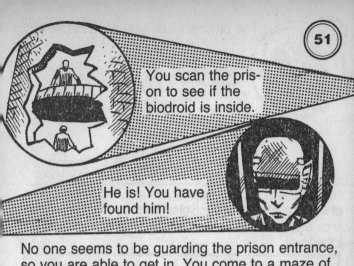

You scan the prison to see if the biodroid is inside.

He is! You have found him!

No one seems to be guarding the prison entrance, so you are able to get in. You come to a maze of circular stone walls. Your scanner shows you two paths. Which way will lead you to the biodroid?

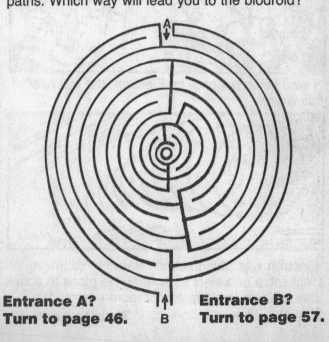

Entrance A?
Turn to page 46.

Entrance B?
Turn to page 57.

The biodroid tells you what happened.

"My mission was to guard the Spy Training Center at Parno. All the other Spies were on a training exercise in another sector. Suddenly the base was attacked!

"I was taken prisoner by Electron, the evil ruler of this world.

"Electron was able to shrink Parno to submicroscopic size and steal its energy. He plans to shrink other planets in his quest for more energy. We must stop him."

Turn to page 47.

You whistle the tune. The door opens! **53**

Quickly you and the biodroid rush out into the corridor. You must get to the tavern and meet the rebels soon.

A warrior sees you! Run!

Turn to page 54.

You run out of the prison. The warriors are close behind.

You climb up steps and get on a moving sidewalk.

There is something wrong! You see rebel citizens and warriors fighting on both sides of the moving sidewalk.

Oh, no! You see another group of warriors on the sidewalk ahead of you. The revolt against Electron has begun! **Go on to the next page.**

Electron's warriors are behind you and in front of you. You must jump off the moving sidewalk and take your chances in one of the battles.

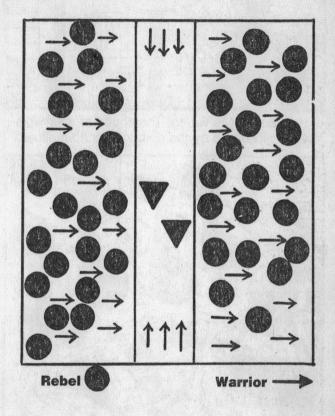

Rebel

Warrior ⟶

Which side has more rebel citizens than warriors? Jump to that side.

Left side? Turn to page 58.

Right side? Turn to page 63.

You whistle the tune.

But something is wrong! The sound of your whistling is picked up by the door lock and amplified.

The sound is amplified a million times. The vibration is more than you can stand. Your bodies begin to shake apart. Music just wasn't one of your talents, Spy! Too bad.

The End

You go through the maze of tunnels. You keep walking and walking until you come to a dead end.

You turn back only to see a wall drop down behind you. You can't get out!

Then the walls on either side of you begin to move toward you. You'll be flat as a pancake in seconds. You hear Electron laughing somewhere nearby. He's calling for syrup.

You leap off the moving sidewalk and into the battle.

You help the rebels fight!

The rebels on this side of the moving sidewalk are winning. The warriors retreat. You go with the rebels to help win the battle on the other side of the walkway.

Turn to page 64.

You tell CEM-450 and the rebels that you will help them defeat Electron. You ask CEM-450 to tell you more about Electron and the microworld.

CEM-450 speaks: "Atomic energy is our food. When Electron came to our planet, he captured our atomic energy reactors. Electron's food is electrical energy. In his floating palace is a converter which he uses to transform our energy into his.

"Electron gives us only enough energy to survive. If we don't obey him, he will cut off our energy food supply. By giving his troops more energy, he has raised a large army of strong warriors."

Turn to page 60.

CEM-450 continues: "Then Electron discovered a gigantic world nearby. He was able to steal all of its energy with his power ray."

CEM-450 resumes: "By using the energy he took from Parno, Electron is building a bigger energy-stealing ray which will work on any planet, near or far. Once the ray is completed, he won't need us anymore. Then he'll finish us off!"

Go on to the next page.

CEM-450 finishes the story: "If only we knew where the giant energy-stealing ray was! All we know is that it is at an energy block connected to both of the city's main power lines. Can you help us?"

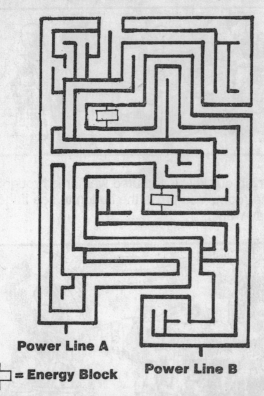

Power Line A

☐— = Energy Block   **Power Line B**

Using your scanner, you quickly analyze the city's two main power lines. You find that there are two energy blocks that seem to be drawing a lot of energy from the power lines. Which power line is connected to both energy blocks?

Power Line A? Turn to page 83.

Power Line B? Turn to page 86.

If Electron's superray is completed, he will have so much energy that he can't be stopped. Hurry!

CEM-450 brings you electrical equipment to construct a ray that will shoot an energy beam in the pattern you chose.

You finish quickly. A captured warrior is brought into the room. You press the button to see if the stun ray works.

Turn to page 74.

You jump off the moving sidewalk to help, but the rebels are outnumbered by Electron's warriors. The battle on this side of the moving sidewalk is quickly over.

The rebels have lost. The warriors surround you. It looks as if you're going to be one of Electron's new pincushions.

The End

You and the rebels quickly fight off the warriors. Then they take you to the Interface Tavern on Romram Street.

CEM-450 has been wounded in the battle, but he is still the leader. He explains that they were fighting the warriors so that they could get you out of prison. You thank the rebels for coming.

In turn, CEM-450 thanks *you* for your help in the fight and then says to all, "We won a small battle today, but Electron is getting more powerful every hour. Perhaps our new friends can help us to regain our planet."

Turn to page 59.

You leave the tavern and rush back to the park where you landed.

Your ship is still there.

You take off and fly toward Electron's floating castle.

Turn to page 66.

As you fly nearer to Electron's castle, you look for a place to hide your ship.

One of the towers is built out of oddly shaped pieces. If one of the pieces matches the shape of your ship, you can hide your ship by attaching it to the wall.

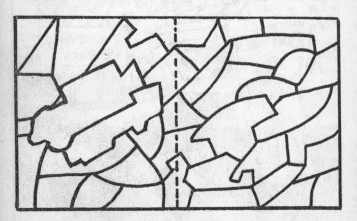

Which side of the wall has a piece that is similar to the shape of the side of your ship?

Right side? Turn to page 73.

Left side? Turn to page 68.

You must think of a way to make up for the weakness of the rebels. Since the micro-worlders have bodies that are similar to computers, there may be a simple way to stun them.

You scan the brain of CEM-450. You find the memory site in the central processor (the brain).

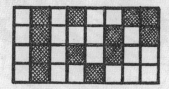

Each part of the pattern is set to on or off. The white parts are on, the black off. If you can turn the on parts off, and the off parts on, you can stun a microworlder. Which of the two patterns below is the opposite of the pattern above?

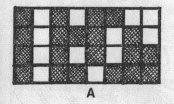

A

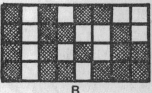

B

Pattern A? Turn to page 62.

Pattern B? Turn to page 71.

68 You find a piece of the wall that matches the shape of your ship. You melt the wall a little so that your ship will fit exactly and not be seen.

No one will find your ship here. You get out and climb to the tower's top.

Go on to the next page.

From the top of the tower, you see a very large garden below you. The only way into the castle is at the other end of the garden.

69

Turn to page 70.

You climb down into the garden.

The garden is bigger than you thought. It is constructed like a maze. Which way to go?

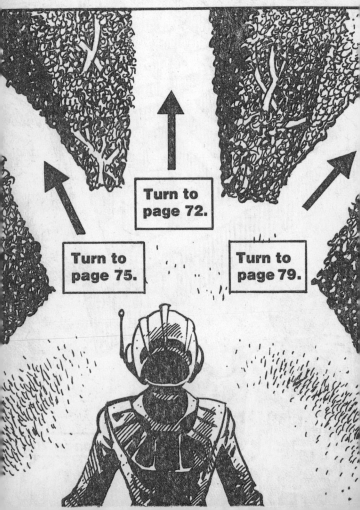

Turn to page 72.

Turn to page 75.

Turn to page 79.

CEM-450 brings you electrical equipment to construct a ray that will shoot an energy beam in the pattern you chose.

71

A captured warrior is brought into the room. You fire the ray at him.

You expect him to be stunned. But the warrior changes shape instead. Your ray has turned him into a monster! Before you can escape, the monster grabs you. You struggle, but your own ray has given him enough power to crush ten Spies!

The End

72 You walk until you see a dangerous-looking animal coming along the path. You decide to hide in the plants.

You try to push your way through the plants, but they won't bend! The animal is getting closer.

Turn to page 84.

You find a piece of the wall that you think matches the shape of your ship. You melt the wall so that your ship will fit. But there's not enough heat, so you try again.

This time you use too much heat. Your ship crashes through the wall! A monster is inside, and it hasn't eaten in a hundred years. Yum!

The End

The captured warrior is stunned! The ray works.

Quickly you show CEM-450 how to build more stun rays. You tell the biodroid to stay with CEM-450 and lead the attack on the giant energy-stealing ray.

It is now time for you to go to Electron's floating castle. By going alone, you may be able to save lives by destroying Electron's energy converter before the rebels attack.

Turn to page 65.

You walk along a garden path, keeping an eye out for danger.

75

Suddenly your motion triggers a plant to attack! You dive out of the way just in time to avoid its sharp spikes!

Turn to page 81.

You walk along the path that was marked "DANGER! KEEP OUT" This may be the only path out of the garden. You hear an evil laugh. Then you see . . .

Electron! He has found you!

Turn to page 80.

Almost too easily, you are able to trap Electron in the vines. You know they won't hold him, but they may give you time to escape.

Electron isn't even struggling. He doesn't seem worried!

Was there something you missed? See if you can find any clues on page 80 and then turn to page 82.

You get through the maze. But you see Electron in front of you! A blast from his trident nearly hits you.

Is he real or not? It doesn't matter because an energy blast will still kill you. You look around for something that might help you defeat Electron.

Are there any plants here that may help you?

Any plants on the left? Turn to page 88.

Any plants on the right? Turn to page 93.

Check pages 75, 84, and the next page if you're not sure.

You walk along the garden path. Suddenly a large plant drops over your head and grabs you!

It tries to trap you in its petals.

But you punch your way out. Another second and its acid juices would have dissolved you.

Turn to page 81.

Electron tries to blast you with his electronic ray.

You see vines growing nearby. Dodging another blast, you pull the vines out of the ground. You must try to tangle up Electron so that you can get away.

Turn to page 77.

You continue to walk through the garden.
The plants are so high that you get lost!

You come to four different paths. One path has a
sign above it. (Check page 16 to see what it says.)
Choose one of the other three paths unless you
are sure where each one goes. Then take the
fourth path, if you dare!

Mark your path in case you come this way again.

You remember that the vines you threw at Electron actually passed *through* his hand and foot!

Suddenly Electron vanishes. You realize that you were looking at a holographic image. The real Electron must be elsewhere.

Look out! Electron's warriors are coming after you!

Turn to page 87.

CEM-450 looks at the map on your scanner. He sends a scout to the energy block location you have chosen.

A few moments pass. The scout returns. But before he can speak, warriors rush in. The scout was followed!

You are surrounded. There is no escape this time, Spy!

84 Your scanner shows you that these plants are made of iron. Their roots go deep into the ground.

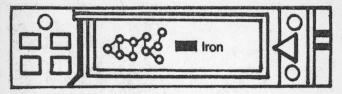

Since you can't push them aside, you quickly climb over them.

You avoid the animal, just in time. Whew!

Turn to page 81.

You run through the maze. A trigger plant almost gets you.

But you are caught by a bell plant.

You try to punch your way out, but you can't!

The End

CEM-450 sends a scout to the energy block you picked. The scout returns a few minutes later. The giant energy-stealing ray is where you said it would be!

You have a double plan. The rebels must destroy the giant energy-stealing ray at once. While they are doing that, you will go alone to Electron's castle. If you can destroy his energy converter, Electron will run out of energy and easily be defeated.

You tell your plan to CEM-450. He says, "We will try, but the warriors have more energy than we do and are stronger."

Turn to page 67.

You run to another part of the garden, checking ahead with your scanner.

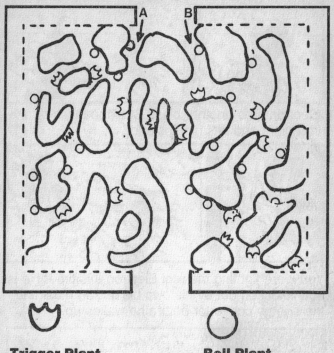

Trigger Plant

Bell Plant

There are two kinds of dangerous plants on the paths ahead of you. One is a deadly trigger plant. You can't go past it *twice* without getting stabbed. The other is the acid bell plant, which will stop you if you go by it only *once*.

Which way should you go?

Entrance A? Turn to page 78.

Entrance B? Turn to page 85.

You recognize an iron plant and hide behind it.

Electron fires another blast. But it bounces off the iron plant and hits him instead!

You were fighting the real Electron this time! He is now knocked out by his own blast. You must find the energy converter before he wakes up.

Look out! Electron's warriors are coming.

Turn to page 96.

You scan the strange-looking plants with your scanner. You learn that if you can find two plants that are exactly the same, you can use their sonic power to blast the guards.

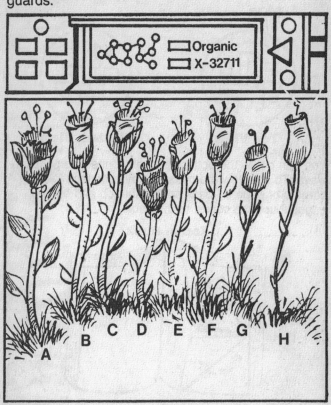

Which two plants are exactly alike?

Plants A and G? Turn to page 100.

Plants B and F? Turn to page 97.

Don't forget to plug up your ears with leaves first!

You must now find Electron's energy converter. By scanning the whole castle, you see that the energy converter is near the bottom of the floating castle. The part of the garden you are in is near the top. Electron's castle is like a giant triangle.

Top View

Bottom View

You can get to the bottom through connecting passageways. To see how the passageways connect, fold the corners of page 91 back so that the top and bottom edges touch the center of the book.

Top of Book

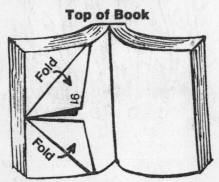

Fold page 91 to find your way through the maze. Which passageway will lead you to the energy converter?

Passage A? Turn to page 99.

Passage B? Turn to page 102.

Fold page 91 back when you are through.

Start Here

A

91

Parno

Energy Converter

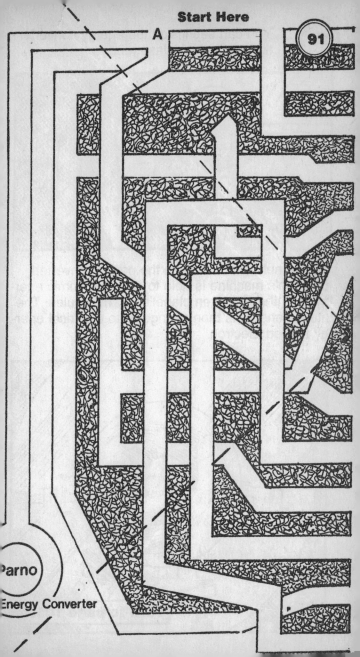

You can see inside the energy converter through a thick glass window.

The planet Parno is inside the power converter! Electron's machine is able to take the atomic energy from the shrunken planet's tiny molecules. The atomic energy is then changed into electrical energy to feed Electron.

Turn to page 101.

You see a control panel nearby that operates the door. If you can make the door open and close very quickly, you can pull your sleeve out. To do this, you must press the buttons in the correct order. These are the buttons on the control panel:

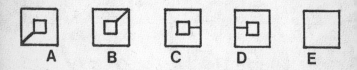

A B C D E

This is the pattern you must follow to shut the door completely

You must fill the pattern in this order by pressing the correct buttons.

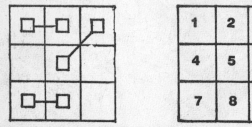

1	2	3
4	5	6
7	8	9

Which is the correct order of buttons to push?

C D A E B E C D E?
Turn to page 103.

C D A E C E B E C?
Turn to page 98.

You tie the ropes together: four ropes at B, three ropes at E, and six ropes at F.

The rebels are hoisted up by the ropes, using the three winches.

The biodroid is first over the railing!

Turn to page 109.

As you run from electron's warriors, you step on a strange-looking plant. It makes a very loud sound that hurts your ears.

Maybe there's a way you can use this plant to help you!

Turn to page 89.

You pull the plants out of the ground and
wrap them together. Then you squeeze
them tightly to force out all their sound.
You aim the plant's cups at the guards.

The sound is so loud that it blasts Electron's
guards! They are stunned by the sonic blast. Good
work, Spy!

**Take the leaves out of your ears and turn
to page 90.**

You punch the buttons. But you made a mistake. The door swings wide open and won't shut.

You are pulled inside! The compressed gravity of Parno is so strong that it drags you into the energy converter. You are crushed!

You crawl through the passageways. You come out in a very large room, full of machinery.

Your scanner tells you that this is Electron's energy converter.

Turn to page 92.

You pull the two plants out of the ground. The sound is nearly deafening.

Then you wrap them together and squeeze!

Blasts of sound come from the two plants. But you didn't choose ones that were *exactly* alike. The sound backfires. You are shattered to pieces by the vibrations.

The End

You see a thick wire inside the energy converter. If you pull it out, the converter will stop and Electron's power will be halted. It may be dangerous, but you've got to take a chance!

You don't have time to figure out how the controls work. You open a small metal door that will allow you to reach inside and pull the wire out.

Your whole body is almost pulled inside by a powerful force! You push back and slam the door. You realize that the converter has a gravity shield. Parno's gravity is strong enough to be dangerous.

You notice that your sleeve is caught in the door. Your *Spy* suit's material is so strong, you can't tear it! If you open the door again, you'll be sucked inside. What can you do?

Turn to page 94.

You climb through a grating and go inside the floating castle, searching for Electron's energy converter.

You crawl through the passageways for a long time. You *should* be getting closer, but you're not sure.

Suddenly you are surrounded by giant rats! You should have gone another way, Spy!

You press the buttons. The door opens and shuts quickly. You pull out your sleeve before you can be sucked inside the energy converter. You are free!

You check your scanner. By now, the biodroid and the rebels should be attacking Electron's giant energy-stealing ray below. You go to a nearby window. Maybe you can see the rebels from here.

Turn to page 105.

"You haven't beaten me yet!" shouts Electron. He laughs and raises his trident.

You turn and look behind you. You see large metal tubes that are used to channel energy beams. If you can get Electron to fire at one of the tubes, the energy will go through the tube and strike him!

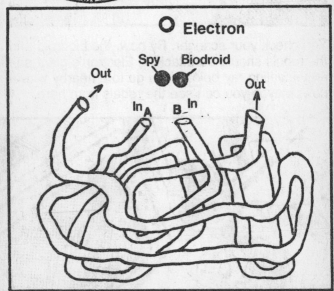

In front of which tube should you stand?

Tube A? Turn to page 113.

Tube B? Turn to page 116.

Be sure to jump out of the way when he fires!

You look through the window. You can see the rebels below.

Using your stun rays, they have successfully captured the giant energy-stealing ray. But you have not yet found a way to turn off the Electron's energy converter.

Just as you are about to go back to the energy converter, you see the biodroid! He is signaling to you in Interplanetary Spy code. The rebels are ready to attack Electron's floating palace.

Turn to page 106.

They need your help to get on board. You open the window, climb out, and get to a railing that circles the palace. Maybe the rebels can help you figure out how to turn off the energy converter safely.

You see piles of ropes, which you can lower to the rebels. Your scanner shows you the distance between the palace and the ground.

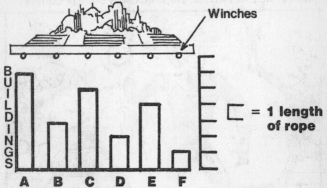

= 1 length of rope

You have thirteen lengths of rope. There are three winches that can be used to pull up the rebels. There are six places where you can move the winches to. Where should you place the winches to use all thirteen lengths of rope?

Places B, E, and F? Turn to page 95.

Places A, E, and B? Turn to page 108.

Electron is still groggy, but he will be fully awake in a few more seconds. You must find a way to stop him. The biodroid still hasn't figured out how to turn off the energy converter.

You must think of something! You quickly remember that when the door to the energy converter was open, the gravitational pull of Parno nearly pulled you inside.

Side View of Door

Top View of Door

You see that the door is attached to a hinge by a screw. If you remove the screw, the door will fall off its hinge. Which way should you turn the screw to pull it out?

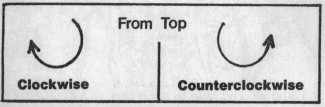

From Top

Clockwise

Counterclockwise

Clockwise? Turn to page 93.

Counterclockwise? Turn to page 110.

Hurry! You must get the door off before Electron knows what you are doing.

You lower the ropes. The rebels grab hold and you pull them up.

You turn around and see that Electron's warriors are coming around the railing from the rear of the castle.

You weren't able to bring up enough rebels in time. Electron's warriors have won!

The End

You, the biodroid, and CEM-450 now are ready to go back to the energy converter to turn it off. The rest of the rebels will attack any of Electron's warriors that they can find on the castle.

When you get back down to the energy converter, you find Electron waiting for you! The power blast he gave himself didn't knock him out long enough.

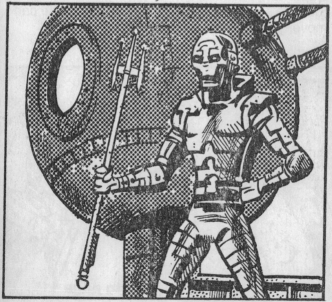

Turn to page 104.

You pull out the screw. You jump out of the way as the little door drops to the ground. The force of Parno's gravity quickly pulls Electron to the energy converter!

Electron's armor plugs up the hole. Before he can move, you grab his trident away from him.

Now he is your prisoner!

Turn to page 115.

Oops! You pull out a bottom rod. A higher rod rolls to the side. Sparks fly. Bolts of pure energy hit the other rods.

Butterfingers! The energy converter blows up!

The writing on the screen says: "TOO FAST!" The biodroid tells you that there is a hatch in the back of the energy converter that can shut it down. Then the room begins to vibrate so much you can't hear his voice.

Since you used Dr. Cyberg's ray to speed yourself up earlier, you now use it to speed yourself up even faster, to match the room's vibrations. You find the hatch and open it.

Turn to page 117.

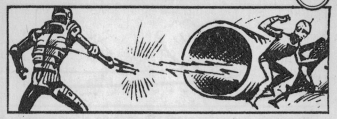

You dodge, and the blast goes into the tube. The energy goes through the tube and zaps Electron!

Electron is knocked out again! Quickly you go to the control panel of the power converter. The biodroid reads the dials.

While the biodroid tries to figure out how to turn the power converter off, you hear Electron moaning. He is waking up!

Turn to page 107.

You pull out the rods very carefully.

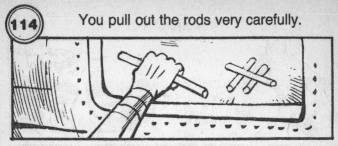

The energy converter stops. Everything slows down again. You slow yourself down so that you can match the speed of CEM-450 and the biodroid.

You have defeated Electron. But again he laughs and says, "You have cut off my source of energy, Spy, but you have also cut off the energy that makes this castle fly." You rush to the window. The castle is falling!

Turn to page 118.

Electron speaks: "You may have captured me, but I'll have my revenge!" He hits a switch on the side of the converter.

The biodroid shouts, "Electron has changed the way the energy converter works. Now most of the energy from Parno is going into the room. Everything will speed up until we explode!"

Can you read what the main screen of the control panel is saying?

Hint: Turn the page sideways and look at it from the edge.

Turn to page 112.

"You have troubled me long enough!" says Electron. He fires.

You jump out of the way. His blast goes into the metal tube. Oh, no! You picked the wrong tube. The blast misses Electron and . . .

hits the energy converter! The energy overloads the circuits. Everything blows up!

KABOOM

The End

Inside the hatch you see atomic rods that control the energy converter. If you can remove the rods, the energy converter will stop working.

Be very careful! You must remove each rod without disturbing any of the other rods. You are looking *down* on the rods. You must pull out the highest rod first, and then the next highest, until they are all gone.

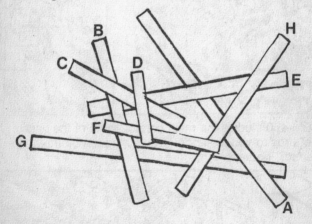

In what order must you pull out the rods?

D C F B H E A G?
Turn to page 114.

D C F H E B G A?
Turn to page 111.

Using the last bit of power from the energy converter, CEM-450 is able to steer the falling castle to a safe landing on top of three strong towers. No one is hurt!

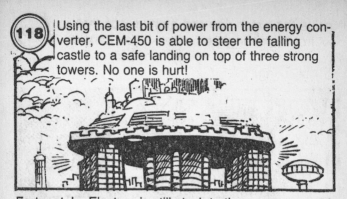

Fortunately, Electron is still stuck to the energy converter. Parno's gravity will hold him there until you are ready to take him to Spy Center for trial.

CEM-450 studies the main control panel of the castle. He turns to you in shock. "Something terrible has happened," he says.

Go on to the next page.

"Electron had used up all the energy in our atomic energy reactors to capture Parno. Now that his converter has been destroyed, there will be no energy for us. Everyone on our planet will die!"

You must think! You can't let a whole planet die. You get an idea. You tell CEM-450 to send for all the people on the planet.

Soon there are thousands of people outside the castle. You are ready to put your plan into action.

Turn to page 120.

You and the biodroid get into your Spy ship. Using Dr. Cyberg's ray, you make your ship bigger.

You get all of the microworlders into your enlarged ship. You put Electron in a tiny cage so you can take him to Spy Center.

You take off into space. You, your ship, and the microworlders get larger and larger. When you are far enough away, you blast the microworld!

Go on to the next page.

The blast destroys the microworld. It also destroys the shielding of the energy converter that was keeping Parno compressed. Parno grows larger again very quickly.

When Parno is large enough, you land. Parno isn't as big as it was, but it is big enough for the enlarged inhabitants of the microworld. Now that they are larger and don't move as fast, they can stop using atomic energy and can use solar-powered energy from Parno's sun.

You say goodbye to CEM-450 and the other microworlders. You radio Spy Center. The biodroid is promoted to a Level 2 Interplanetary Spy. You defeated Electron and saved *two* planets. Well done, Interplanetary Spy!

The End

BE AN INTERPLANETARY SPY